COUNTY CUP 1

CUP FAVOURITES

Also available by Rob Childs,
and published by Corgi Yearling Books:

County Cup series
1: CUP FAVOURITES
2: CUP RIVALS

Coming soon:
3. CUP SHOCKS
4. CUP CLASHES

Soccer Mad series
FOOTBALL FANATIC
SOCCER MAD
ALL GOALIES ARE CRAZY
FOOTBALL DAFT
FOOTBALL FLUKES
SOCCER STARS

SOCCER MAD COLLECTION
includes SOCCER MAD, ALL GOALIES ARE CRAZY

SOCCER AT SANDFORD
SANDFORD ON TOUR

Published by Young Corgi Books:

The Big series

THE BIG GAME
THE BIG MATCH
THE BIG PRIZE
THE BIG DAY
THE BIG KICK
THE BIG GOAL
THE BIG WIN

THE BIG CLASH
THE BIG BREAK
THE BIG CHANCE
THE BIG STAR
THE BIG FREEZE
THE BIG FIX
THE BIG DROP

THE BIG FOOTBALL COLLECTION
includes THE BIG GAME, THE BIG MATCH, THE BIG PRIZE

THE BIG FOOTBALL FEAST
includes THE BIG DAY, THE BIG KICK, THE BIG GOAL

THE BIG FOOTBALL TREBLE
Includes THE BIG BREAK, THE BIG CHANCE, THE BIG STAR

Published by Corgi Pups,
for beginner readers:

GREAT SAVE!
GREAT SHOT!

ROB CHILDS

COUNTY CUP

Book One
The North Quarter

Cup Favourites

Illustrated by Robin Lawrie

CORGI YEARLING BOOKS

CUP FAVOURITES
A CORGI YEARLING BOOK : 978 0 440 87087 6

First publication in Great Britain

PRINTING HISTORY
Corgi Yearling edition published 2000

7 9 10 8 6

Copyright © 2000 by Rob Childs
Illustrations copyright © 2000 by Robin Lawrie

The right of Rob Childs to be identified as the author of this work
has been asserted in accordance with the Copyright, Designs
and Patents Act, 1988

Set in 12/15 New Century Schoolbook by
Phoenix Typesetting, Ilkley, West Yorkshire.

Corgi Yearling Books are published by Transworld Publishers,
61-63 Uxbridge Road, London W5 5SA,
a division of The Random House Group Ltd
Addresses for companies within The Random House Group Limited can be found at:
www.randomhouse.co.uk/offices.htm

The Random House Group Limited supports The Forest Stewardship
Council® (FSC®), the leading international forest-certification organisation.
Our books carrying the FSC label are printed on FSC®-certified paper.
FSC is the only forest-certification scheme supported by the leading
environmental organisations, including Greenpeace. Our
paper procurement policy can be found at
www.randomhouse.co.uk/environment

MIX
Paper from
responsible sources
FSC® C018072

Printed and bound in Great Britain by Clays Ltd, St Ives plc

INTRODUCTION

L ong ago, the historic county of Medland was made up of four separate regions. These divisions can now only be found on ancient maps, but people living in the old North, South, East and West Quarters still remain loyal to their own area.

One way that the traditional rivalry between the Quarters is kept up is by means of the County Cup.

Every year, schools from all over the county take part in this great soccer tournament and the standard of football is always high. Matches are played on a local group basis at first to decide the Quarter Champions, who will then clash in the knockout stages of the competition later in the season.

The winners receive the much-prized silver trophy and earn the right to call themselves the County Champions – the top team in Medland.

THE COUNTY OF MEDLAND

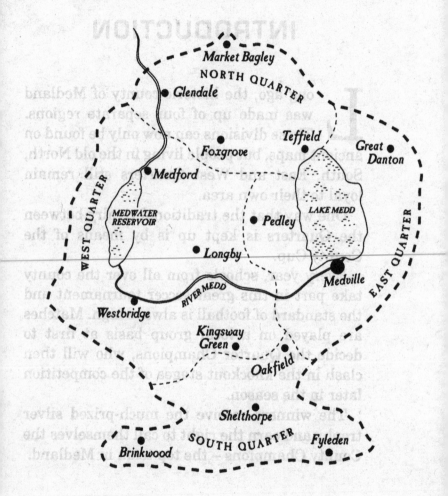

SCHOOLS

These are the sixteen schools that have qualified to play in the County Cup this season – try and see where they are on the map . . .

NORTH QUARTER

Foxgrove High School
Glendale Community School
Market Bagley Community School
Teffield Comprehensive School

EAST QUARTER

Great Danton High School
Lakeview High School, Medville
Medville Comprehensive School
Sir George Needham Community College, Pedley

SOUTH QUARTER

Fyleden Community College
Oakfield High School
Shelthorpe Comprehensive School
St Wystan's Comprehensive School, Brinkwood

WEST QUARTER

Hillcrest Comprehensive School, Longby
Kingsway Green High School
Riverside Comprehensive School, Medford
Westbridge Community College

FOXGROVE

GLENDALE

GREAT DANTON

LAKEVIEW

FYLEDEN

OAKFIELD

HILLCREST

KINGSWAY GREEN

MARKET BAGLEY

TEFFIELD

MEDVILLE

SIR GEORGE NEEDHAM

SHELTHORPE

ST WYSTAN

RIVERSIDE

WESTBRIDGE

Blandale Community School

Trafford Comprehensive School

Foxgrove High School

Market Bagley Community School

MEET THE TEAMS

A bright, breezy Saturday morning in early October sees the start of the County Cup competition in the North Quarter of Medland. Four teams in the under-12 age-group will be battling it out between now and Christmas in the hope of becoming Quarter Champions.

The opening fixtures in the round-robin group are:

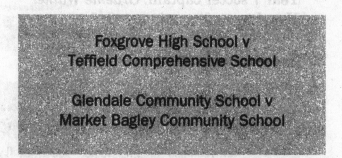

Foxgrove High School v
Teffield Comprehensive School

Glendale Community School v
Market Bagley Community School

Meet the teams on the next few pages and perhaps even choose one that you might like to support in their games. Then follow their fortunes in this book to see what happens in the exciting quest for the County Cup.

Who will be Champions of the North?

Read on and find out . . .

FOXGROVE HIGH SCHOOL

Medium-sized secondary school in the village of Foxgrove in the North Quarter, with pupils in year groups 7, 8 and 9 only, aged between 11 and 14.

Headteacher: *Mr John Wright*

Teacher in charge of year 7 soccer: *Mr Ray Norton*

School colours: *gold shirts, black shorts, gold socks*

Year 7 soccer captain: *Graeme Walker*

Usual team formation: *4–3–3*

Year 7 soccer squad:

Matthew Reynolds (Bread Roll)

Sanjay Thakrar   Adam Johnson   Sam Spencer   Andrew Cobb

Ben Yeomans   Graeme Walker   Joe Lynex (Lynx)

Clayton Fraser   Mike Jesson   Will Harrison

plus:

Mark Peters, Zahir Aziz (Zed), Gary Aimsley, Barry Donaldson (Baz), Rajesh Parmar, Ian Swann, Craig Allen

10

Notes...

This is going to be our year. Our name's on the County Cup already – or at least that's what Matt says. He's the Foxes super-confident keeper and hates letting any goals in. He gets dead mad when it happens and blames everybody but himself. Typical!

Most of us went to Foxgrove Primary and so we've been playing together for years. Shows in our team-work. That must make us favourites to retain the Quarter Shield the High School won last season – and then who's going to stop us after that? Answer – nobody!

Mike will sure take some stopping. He's a real goal-grabber and was leading scorer in the primary league. I like to get my name on the scoresheet, too, and Matt reckons I've got the hardest shot he's ever faced.

Lynx makes a lot of our goals with his deadly accurate left-foot passes and corners, and watch out for the pace of Clayton on the right wing. He's lightning fast. Nobody else has a chance in the sprint races on Sports Day. No doubt about it. Matt's right – Foxes for the Cup!

GLENDALE COMMUNITY SCHOOL

Large comprehensive school in market town of Glendale in the North Quarter.

Headteacher: *Mrs Margaret Burrows*
Head of P.E. Dept: *Mr Brian Fisher*
School colours: *royal blue shirts, shorts and socks*
Year 7 soccer captain: *Paul Stevens*
Usual team formation: *4–2–4*

Year 7 soccer squad:

Ian Jacobs (Crackers)
(Batty) (Dips)
Robbie Jones   Paul Stevens   Tom Bateman   Dipesh Patel

Hanif Khan   Alex Wainwright (Wainy)

Nick Green   Harry Taylor   Chris Kemp   Tim Lamb
(Giant) (Leggy)

plus:

Scott Harris, Carl Simpson, Jeff Smith, David Nash, Richard Curtis, Gary Thomas

12

I reckon we've got a pretty good chance in the County Cup with such a strong squad. We're a very attacking team with goals likely to come from anywhere. Even Crackers, our keeper, netted a penalty recently! Giant got over thirty goals for his primary school last season, mostly headers because of his size. He's deadly in the air and makes a great target man for our fast wingers, Nick and Leggy.

Kempy is our other main striker, but sometimes he drops into midfield when we switch to 4-3-3 or we bring in hard-man Carl or perhaps Nashy to play there instead. Nashy's useful in goal too so that helps to keep Crackers on his toes.

It's usually left to Batty and me to try and hold the defence together, which isn't easy to do when we go on all-out attack! No wonder Mr Fisher's nearly bald. He must have torn out most of his hair watching people like us let too many stupid goals in! Hope you'll support us in our matches and help Glendale to win the Cup. I promise you plenty of excitement along the way!

Large comprehensive school in the market town of the same name in the far north of the county.

Headteacher: *Mr Stephen Gray*
P.E. teacher: *Mr Roger Knight*
School colours: *All-white with red trim and red socks*
Year 7 soccer captain: *Duncan Bell*
Usual team formation: *sweeper system*

Year 7 soccer squad:

Colin Deacon

Duncan Bell (Ding-Dong)
(O.K.)
Guy Mansel   Oliver Kane   Paul Sturgess

(Charlie) Jason Chaplin   Timothy Day(Half-Day)

Geraint Evans   David Young

Luke Wilde   Daniel West

plus:

Michael Richards, Ryan Cook, Robert Ireland, Lee Tomlinson, Thomas Fletcher, Chris Lowe

Notes...

Hi! My name's Duncan Bell. Or it was till I started at the Comp and O.K. (that's Oliver, our centre-back) thought the captain ought to have a nickname, too, like him and 'Charlie' Chaplin. Now nearly everybody calls me Ding-Dong.

Names can be a bit weird, I guess. We have to call our P.E. teacher Sir, but it suits him as he's a Knight. (We've also got a Day in our squad, sometimes known as Half-Day since he fell asleep one afternoon in maths!) O.K. reckons Sir only picks Luke and Dan up front together in attack so he can write Wilde West on the teamsheet!

Even the team has a nickname - the Baggies. We quite fancy our chances this term in the County Cup, but we know we're up against some tough opposition. We've made a decent start to the season, winning two of our first three league games, with me playing as sweeper in Sir's favourite defensive system. Seems to be working well so far, as it gives Charlie and Half-Day more freedom to move forward and join in attacks like wing-backs.

Wish us luck - we'll probably need it!

TEFFIELD COMPREHENSIVE SCHOOL

Small comprehensive school in the town of Teffield near Lake Medd in the North Quarter.

Headteacher: *Miss Jane Robertson*
P.E. teacher: *Mr Jeff Pearson*
School colours: *green-and-white striped shirts, green shorts & socks*
Year 7 soccer captain: *Jack Whitehead*
Usual team formation: *4–4–2*

Year 7 soccer squad:

Philip Clarke (Pip)

Joseph French   Bryn Davies   Gary Field   Liam Hunter

(Duncan)   Martin Reid   Nazir Hussein
David Edwards   Danny Gregson

Jack Whitehead   Andy Turner

plus:

Neil Simms, Mark Chivers, James Docherty (Mac), Denis Ingham

16

Mr Pearson's told me to write a couple of hundred words about our football team and how we want to win the County Cup this season. He'll be lucky. I'll have writer's cramp by the end of it. He'll have to check my spelling as well because writing stuff down isn't exactly my strong point. Actions speak louder than words, as the saying goes. That's the way I like to captain sides - leading by example on the pitch, not by talking. I play up front with Andy and we make a kind of twin spearhead for the team. We also have a friendly rivalry over who's going to be top scorer for Teffield this season.

Not sure what else to write really. I mean, we'd like to do well in the competition, but we're the smallest school in our group so we don't have as many kids to pick from as the others. But you can be sure of one thing at least. We'll all be giving it our best shot every match - especially me and Andy in attack - right into the back of the net. There, finished at last! Not bad, eh? I make that dead on 200 words!

FOXGROVE v TEFFIELD

Saturday 4 October
k.o. 9.45 a.m.
Referee: Mr R. Norton

. . . let's join the match at a key moment midway through the second half – it looks like the Foxes leading scorer is just about to shoot . . .

'GGOOAALL!'

Mike Jesson let out his usual whoop of delight. It was a war cry that had often echoed around the school playing fields since the start of term. The goal was his second of the game and his tenth of the season already.

His teammates ran up to perform their new goal celebration dance. They grouped themselves behind the scorer, bending low as if sniffing the ground, and zigzagged after him towards the halfway line. The teacher didn't approve of such a spectacle, but Graeme Walker, the Foxes captain, claimed that it only reflected the team's nickname.

'The scorer's the fox and the rest are the chasing pack of hounds,' he'd explained to Mr

Norton the previous week after its first public display. 'He's dodging about trying to put them off the scent so he can get away.'

Mike was making no great effort to escape the pack's attentions. He was soon caught and dragged down beneath a pile of writhing bodies.

'Great stuff!' Graeme screamed into his pal's ear. '3–0 – that's clinched it for sure.'

Mike grinned up at him. 'Yeah, Teffield are dead meat now.'

There was still a little life left in the corpse, however. The boys of Teffield Comprehensive were not ready to lie down and die with their legs in the air – not unless it was some daft routine of their own that they'd been practising. The visitors were just as keen as the Foxes to enjoy a good run in the County Cup competition. And so were their parents on the touchline.

'C'mon, Teffield, get stuck in,' shouted one of them. 'You gave 'em that goal. Where was the marking?'

'That bloke's not a very happy bunny!' Graeme laughed as he waited for the game to restart. 'He's been moaning away like that all match.'

His midfield partner, Lynx, pulled a face. 'He always does.'

'You know him?'

Lynx nodded. 'Liam, their number three, plays for my Sunday team and that's his dad. We call him the Medd!'

The captain looked puzzled. 'Why the Medd?'

''Cos he's got a mouth as big as the lake!'

The Teffield players didn't need any kiss of life from the Medd's gaping mouth to spark their revival. It was their own bruised pride and their captain Jack Whitehead that drove them forward on to the attack again in search of a goal that might bring them back into the game.

Jack clipped the bar with a superb effort from outside the penalty area and they laid siege to the home side's goal for the next five minutes. They forced three successive corners, all taken by the captain himself, and the Foxes keeper had to be at his most alert to keep them at bay.

'Saved, Matt!' cried Graeme as the keeper pushed a close-range shot round the post for yet another corner. 'Good job you got down to that one. Would have gone in.'

'No sweat,' Matt replied. 'They won't get past me today.'

Famous last words. The ball sailed over to the far post this time and was met by a soaring leap from the Teffield number nine, Andy Turner. Matt was left flat-footed by the power and placement of the header. The ball rocketed into the opposite corner of the goal and only ended up in his arms as it bounced back out of the net.

There were no over-the-top celebrations from the modest scorer. Andy simply collected the ball from the astonished goalkeeper and ran back to the halfway line to place it on the centre spot. He didn't want to give Foxgrove any excuse to delay the kick-off.

'About time too!' yelled the Medd. 'C'mon, let's have another goal.'

His wish was soon granted, but not quite in the way intended. It was the Foxes' turn to win a corner and Lynx curled it tantalizingly into the goalmouth. In the untidy scramble that resulted, one shot hit a post, another was blocked on the line and then Liam sliced the ball into his own net.

Liam sank to his knees in despair and it took a few seconds for the Medd to realize what had happened. When he did, he let rip a terrible torrent of abuse, mostly directed at his embarrassed son.

'Poor kid,' grunted Graeme as Liam's teammates helped the unlucky defender back to his feet. 'Fancy having a dad like that.'

The Teffield teacher intervened and led the man away towards the car park to try and calm him down. Neither of them saw any more of the match, which continued in a strange, hushed atmosphere after the outburst. Mr Norton was relieved to blow the final whistle.

'Well done, lads, a fine win, but that's only the start,' he told his players as they briefly gathered round the referee before going in to change. 'There's a long way to go yet in this competition so don't go getting carried away.'

That's exactly what Mike Jesson did. He

completely failed to heed the teacher's warning and jumped up on Graeme's back as they set off for the school building.

'*We're gonna win the Cup! We're gonna win the Cup!*' he chanted tunelessly as Graeme protested beneath his weight.

'Get off, will yer, you great lump. You heard what Norton said. We've still got another two group games to play.'

'No trouble. We're easily the best team in the north,' Mike boasted, dismounting.

'What about Glendale?'

'Nah – rubbish! We beat them 4–2 last month and I got a hat-trick!'

'Thought you might mention that,' laughed the captain. 'But that was only a friendly. They'll be out for revenge when we meet them in the Cup.'

'Can't wait. I'll grab another hat-trick then as well.'

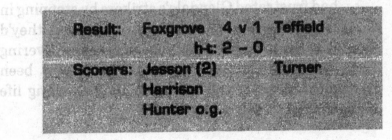

Result:	Foxgrove	4 v 1	Teffield
		h-t: 2 – 0	
Scorers:	Jesson (2)		Turner
	Harrison		
	Hunter o.g.		

GLENDALE v MARKET BAGLEY

Saturday 4 October
k.o. 10 a.m.
Referee: Mr B. Fisher

. . . meanwhile, due to a later kick-off, there are still ten minutes left to play in the other opening game. By the time the Foxes are singing in the showers, Glendale are staring defeat in the face – 2–1 down at home to the Baggies . . .

'**P**layed, Ding-Dong,' called out the Baggies keeper, Colin Deacon, as his captain intercepted the ball and passed it out to one of their wing-backs.

Duncan 'Ding-Dong' Bell was having an inspired game as sweeper. Time and again, he had frustrated Glendale's strikers by stepping in to clear the danger when it appeared they'd found a path through to goal. He was covering the main markers superbly, as if he'd been playing the sweeper role all his footballing life instead of only a few weeks.

Duncan had even taken the chance before the interval to stride forward out of defence and set up his team's equalizer. When this was followed by another goal inside a minute, both scored by Luke Wilde, Glendale were in disarray. And their second half performance so far had been little better.

Mr Fisher, Glendale's P.E. teacher and referee, decided that it was time to take a gamble. He blew his whistle to stop the action and signalled to the substitutes on the touchline.

'Carl, get that top off, you're coming on in midfield,' he ordered. 'We'll switch to a 4–3–3 line-up, lads. See if that'll make any difference.'

Carl Simpson swaggered on to the pitch, his sleeves already rolled up to the elbows as usual to show everyone that he meant business.

'Right let's sort this lot out now I'm on,' he demanded. 'They're sure gonna know I'm around.'

The first opponent that Carl introduced himself to was Luke. As the goalscorer received a pass in the centre-circle, Carl arrived too, lunging in from behind with no real intention of winning the ball. The reckless challenge dumped Luke on the ground, clutching his ankle in pain.

'Dirty foul, referee!' shouted the boy's mother. 'Send him off!'

'Steady, Carl,' the teacher warned him after awarding the free-kick. 'We don't want anybody getting hurt.'

Carl turned away and sneered to himself. 'Huh! That's what you think.'

The substitute soon picked out his next target, the Baggies captain. Carl was a stocky, muscular boy, very much the opposite of the slender Duncan, and when the two of them collided in mid-air as they jumped for a cross the outcome was a foregone conclusion.

'You OK, Ding-Dong?' asked his goalkeeper, helping him to sit up.

'Think I've just been hit by a jumbo jet,' he mumbled, winded.

'Close,' said Colin. 'It was that crazy elephant wearing number thirteen. He's a nutter!'

The free-kick for the foul on the captain was wasted, the ball given away carelessly to Glendale's lanky left-winger.

'Take that kid on, Leggy,' hollered Carl. 'Go on, skin him alive!'

Tim Lamb loved the chance to run at defenders, using his long legs to outpace them once he'd tricked his way past. On this occasion, he simply pushed the ball up the touchline and ran, leaving his marker for dead. Duncan was still too dazed to react to the danger and the winger had time to look up, steady himself and hit over a perfect high centre.

It landed smack on the head of the tallest person on the pitch. Harry Taylor was even bigger than the referee and fully merited the nickname of Giant. Nobody else could get near the ball and he buried his header into the top corner of the net, well beyond Colin's despairing dive.

Giant was mobbed by his relieved teammates. It wasn't the first time this season that his height had come to their rescue when all seemed lost. And no doubt it wouldn't be the last either.

'We were robbed!' cried one of the visiting supporters as the teams left the pitch shortly afterwards. 'You didn't deserve to get a draw.'

The Glendale players ignored the taunt. They were just grateful to have salvaged a precious point.

Result:	Glendale 2 v 2 Market Bagley	
	h-t: 1 – 2	
Scorers:	Khan	Wilde (2)
	Taylor	

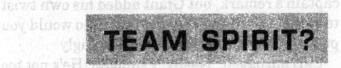

TEAM SPIRIT?

... pull up a chair at one of the dinner tables in Glendale School's canteen on Monday and listen to what's being said about the Cup match ...

'You were rubbish, Crackers!' Carl sneered. 'My granny could've saved them two goals you let in.'

The goalkeeper glanced up from his meal. 'I didn't know your granny liked playing in goal,' he replied. 'Good, is she?'

'Don't try and be clever with me. I'll do you.'

'You're always going to *do* somebody, aren't you, Carl? I've only known you a few weeks and I must have heard you say that a million times.'

'So? Look at the way I *did* some of them Baggies. Soon showed 'em who was boss,' he boasted. 'You lot were just letting 'em walk all over you. It's only thanks to me we got a draw out of that game.'

Paul Stevens cut in. 'Nothing to do with Leggy's magic cross, then, and Giant's un-stoppable header?'

Carl failed to pick up the sarcasm in the captain's remark, but Giant added his own twist to it. 'So apart from your granny, who would you put in goal instead?' he asked teasingly.

Carl shrugged. 'Nashy, I suppose. He's not too bad.'

'Better than Crackers here, you think?'

'Said so, didn't I?' he snarled, hating the way the other players were smirking, as if making fun of him. 'No way they should've scored twice against us.'

'Blame the whole defence, then, not just Crackers,' Paul told him. 'Blame me. I was marking the kid who got the goals.'

He let the challenge dangle in the air between them, but Carl at least had the sense to know that threatening the captain wasn't the best way of earning himself a regular place in the side.

'Got to go,' Carl muttered instead, scraping his chair across the floor as he stood up. 'Fisher wants to see me.'

'Now I wonder what that could be about?' Crackers piped up as Carl turned away. 'You committing GBH on the Baggies, maybe?'

Carl could hear the sniggers behind him as he stormed out of the hall. 'I'll do him for that later,' he promised himself. 'I'll do the lot of 'em!

About time they gave me some respect.'

'Glad he's gone,' said Hanif Khan, the scorer of their first goal in the Cup. 'He really gets on my nerves. Hope Fisher does have a go at him.'

'Yeah, serve him right. Give him a taste of his own medicine for a change,' said Wainy, Hanif's partner in midfield. 'He's always having a go at me.'

'Who, Fisher?'

'No, stupid! Carl. Just 'cos I'm small.'

'He ought to pick on people his own size,' put in Giant and then wondered why they were all laughing.

'Good job you're not a bully, then, Giant,' said Hanif. 'There'd be nobody else around for you to pick on!'

Paul took up the point more seriously, concerned about Carl's effect on team spirit. 'I didn't know Carl was giving you a hard time, Wainy.'

'Oh, started years ago,' he said wearily. 'You guys are lucky. You didn't have to suffer him at primary school too like I did.'

'Poor old you,' said Crackers, finishing his meal. 'He wants locking up, if you ask me. 'He's a real head-case.'

'I should watch out for him now,' Wainy

warned him. 'Carl won't forget what you said earlier. He bears grudges.'

'I can look after myself, don't worry. And anway, if he does give me any grief, I can always set Giant on to him!'

As they got up to leave, chuckling, the captain sensed they had a possible problem on their hands. Carl's physical approach might well have worked to their advantage on Saturday, but Paul was uneasy about the prospect of having him rampaging around the pitch all the time.

'I don't want people to think we're just a bunch of dirty foulers,' he sighed. 'I'd rather we lost trying to play good football than kick our way through the County Cup!'

. . . hmm . . . wonder what you think about how Glendale's captain feels? . . .

WILDE-WEST SHARPSHOOTERS

*... better check on how the Baggies are preparing
for their next Cup game ...*

'Fantastic shot, Dan!' cried Duncan 'Ding-
Dong' Bell. 'Right through the smallest
hoop without even touching it. Dead
centre.'

Daniel West grinned at his captain. 'Six-
pointer, that is. Puts me in the lead.'

Six hoops were suspended from a crossbar for
target practice. The smaller the hoop, the more
it was worth.

'Your turn, O.K.,' said Duncan, nodding across
to his centre-back. 'C'mon, aim for that big one
in the top corner.'

Oliver Kane hadn't yet managed to score a
single point. He'd only just returned from
another trek into the long grass to retrieve his
ball and now dribbled it into the penalty area,
setting himself up for the shot.

'Shoot!'

The ball sailed over the crossbar and the whole group collapsed with laughter. 'Not again!' he wailed.

'Get mine as well while you're there, O.K., will you?' called out their goalkeeper. Colin was taking the chance to practise his own rusty shooting skills and his latest effort had flown well wide of the goal.

'Fat chance!' Oliver retorted. 'Fetch it yourself.'

As Oliver trudged off, Duncan himself prepared to let fly. He was more fortunate. His shot passed between two of the hoops, but at least it was accurate enough to go in the goal and the net saved him a journey.

'How many points you got, Ding-Dong?' Dan asked.

'Ten. Same as Luke.'

Luke Wilde was running in now, the ball under full control as he looked up to pick his next target – the hoop hanging by the left-hand post. It was a careful, sidefoot effort,

but the ball curled away, struck the post and rebounded to his feet. Instinctively, he crashed it goalwards again and this time the ball flashed through a different hoop into the net.

'Yeesss!' he shrieked. 'That's another four.'

'No way!' cried Dan. 'Rebounds don't count, Sir said.'

Luke and Dan were the Baggies' Wilde-West strike partnership, each keen to finish the season as the team's top scorer. Luke was leading 7–4 at the moment after five matches, including his two Cup goals against Glendale.

'They ought to be worth double,' he replied. 'All great goalscorers need quick reflexes. Give them half a chance and the ball's in the back of the net. Just like my winner last week in the league.'

Dan pulled a face. 'A lucky deflection, that's all. It was a brilliant header from me.'

'Rubbish! Keeper would've saved it, if I hadn't got that little touch.'

'Just hit you on the shoulder.'

'So what! Doesn't matter where . . .'

'Belt up, you two!' ordered Duncan. 'Your go again, Dan.'

The striker was confident enough to shoot from only just inside the area, but the ball veered wide. He trotted after it, trying hard to ignore Luke's jeers.

Their P.E. teacher, Mr Knight, left a group practising their heading to check on the progress of the shooters.

'Right, who's got the most points so far?' he asked.

'Give you two guesses, Sir,' laughed Duncan.

The captain's response highlighted the very problem that the teacher was trying to tackle. The team tended to rely too heavily on Luke and Dan for their goals. Hardly anyone else had scored yet in their matches.

The players reported their tally and Mr Knight watched them in action for a while, making coaching points to improve their accuracy. By the time he wandered away, even Oliver had opened his account.

Although the Baggies' league results had been good, with Colin keeping two clean sheets on the trot, Mr Knight knew they would have to start scoring more goals to have any chance of winning the County Cup. The big test was soon to come. Their next match was at home to the Foxes.

'That's the crunch game,' he mused. 'Beat them and we'll go top of the group. But if we lose, we're out!'

. . . what's your shooting like? You might well benefit from a session with the County Coach . . .

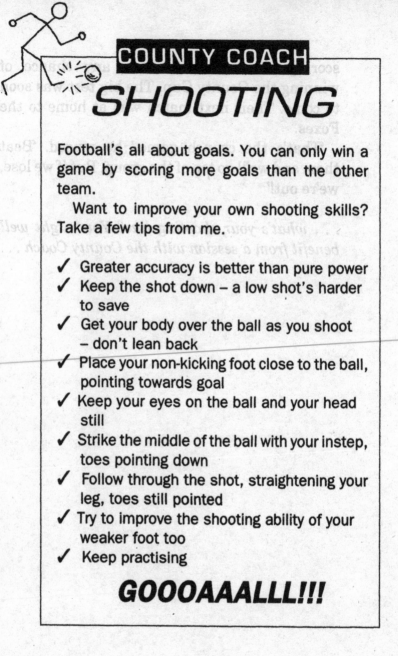

COUNTY COACH

SHOOTING

Football's all about goals. You can only win a game by scoring more goals than the other team.

Want to improve your own shooting skills? Take a few tips from me.

- ✓ Greater accuracy is better than pure power
- ✓ Keep the shot down – a low shot's harder to save
- ✓ Get your body over the ball as you shoot – don't lean back
- ✓ Place your non-kicking foot close to the ball, pointing towards goal
- ✓ Keep your eyes on the ball and your head still
- ✓ Strike the middle of the ball with your instep, toes pointing down
- ✓ Follow through the shot, straightening your leg, toes still pointed
- ✓ Try to improve the shooting ability of your weaker foot too
- ✓ Keep practising

GOOOAAALLL!!!

MARKET BAGLEY v FOXGROVE

Saturday 25 October
k.o. 10 a.m.
Referee: Mr R. Knight

. . . no goals yet, ten minutes into the match, but it surely can't be long before they start coming – the Baggies' sweeper system is breaking down . . .

'**G**et a grip on that kid, Half-Day,' shouted Duncan. 'He's running riot.'

'Huh! I'll get a grip on him all right in a minute – round his neck!' muttered the defender. 'Problem is, I'll have to catch him first.'

Tim Day, Half-Day to his teammates, was struggling. He had never come up against anyone as fast as the Foxes tall, black right-winger. Every time the ball came their way, the winger's explosive pace exposed Half-Day's lack of it, and the captain was kept busy sweeping up behind him.

Duncan's services were in demand elsewhere too. He found himself having to try and plug other holes in his leaking defence opened up by the visitors' tidal wave of attacks. Only Colin's acrobatics in goal had so far saved the Baggies from embarrassment.

'C'mon, men, mark up tight. I can't be in three places at once,' the captain complained, red in the face. 'They're all over us like a swarm of bees.'

Perhaps it was Foxgrove's black and gold kit that brought the analogy to mind, but they had no time to dwell upon it. The bees were stinging again, bringing fresh torment to Half-Day. The winger showed him the ball then surged past and whipped a low cross into the middle before the sweeper could respond.

Duncan's rival captain caught the ball on the volley just inside the penalty area. Graeme Walker's fierce strike defeated Colin's dive, but this time the woodwork came to the keeper's rescue. The ball smacked against the crossbar with the force of a thunderclap and the rebound was booted away upfield in relief.

The hefty clearance took the Foxes by surprise. The Baggies launched a sudden, break-away raid, two on to one, with Luke in possession and Dan sprinting free, unmarked.

'Chop him down, Bread Roll!' screamed Matt from his goal.

It was too late. The lone defender, Andrew

Cobb, had played both attackers onside, but he wasn't close enough to either of them to make a tackle, fair or otherwise. Luke dragged him out wide then unselfishly switched the ball inside to Dan who was in the clear.

'Offside, ref!' appealed the Foxes supporters, but Mr Knight waved play on.

Dan hesitated for a moment, expecting the whistle, then concentrated on the task in hand. This was somewhat more difficult than trying to score through hoops. He was now faced by a goalkeeper who was hurtling towards him to narrow the angle.

Dan usually preferred to shoot rather than dribble round the keeper in these situations, but the boy was advancing so quickly that the striker tried to sell him a dummy with a little body swerve. Matt wasn't tricked into buying. He timed his dive expertly and wrapped both arms around the ball to send Dan toppling over, full-length. The chance had vanished.

'Idiot! Why didn't you pass to me?' Luke yelled in frustration.

Dan was too winded to answer him back. He just sat on the grass, feeling sorry for himself.

Amazingly, the deadlock wasn't broken until almost the last kick of the first half. As Clayton

Fraser, the Foxes number seven, burst into the box once more, a stumbling Half-Day stretched out a leg in desperation and brought him crashing down.

'Penalty!'

Mr Knight could not ignore this loud chorus of appeals. He had no choice but to point to the spot.

There seemed to be a brief dispute about who was going to take the penalty before the captain strode forward with the ball under his arm. Graeme's technique was to blast it as hard as possible, relying on sheer power to beat the goalie. Colin threw himself to his left, but only succeeded in making it look as if he was diving out of the line of fire. If he had stayed where he was, the cannonball might have drilled a hole through his chest.

The two team camps shared a feeling of disbelief during the interval. The Baggies couldn't believe how badly they had played, and the Foxes were trying to work out how they had only managed a single goal.

'Should have had at least six by now,' muttered Mike Jesson, their leading scorer. 'And I'm just talking about me.'

'You're not kiddin',' laughed Clayton. 'The number of times me and Lynx have dropped the ball on that big head of yours!'

'Soz about the pen,' said Graeme, wrapping an arm round Mike's shoulders. 'I just think it's a captain's responsibility, that's all.'

'Thought we'd agreed to take them in turns this season. You took that one we had a few weeks ago.'

Graeme grinned. 'I'll take the next one too. My job, OK? You get enough goals as it is.'

'Not today, I don't. They just won't go in,' he moaned.

Mr Norton, their teacher, overheard. 'Be patient, Mike. You can't score every time. The main thing is that we're creating the chances. That's more than they're doing.'

'Yeah, I'm getting bored,' Matt chipped in. 'And cold. Only had that one save to make.'

'Just keep playing the way you are doing and the goals are bound to come,' the teacher told them. 'Get the ball out to Clayton as much as possible. Their full-back doesn't know what day it is.'

As far as Tim was concerned, it was half-day closing. He was substituted, but his replacement also found Clayton too hot to handle. Both the second-half goals came from Clayton's crosses. One was turned in by Lynx at the far post and the other was finished off by Mike at last finding the net with a bullet header.

'GOOAALL!!' he cried, racing off to leap into Clayton's bear hug in excitement. This was followed by the Foxes' well-rehearsed pack of hounds routine as his teammates scuttled after the scorer back to the centre-circle. Even Matt sprinted the length of the field to join in and warm himself up.

Mr Norton sighed. 'There they go again with that stupid dance. I think I might have to put a ban on fox hunting before too long!'

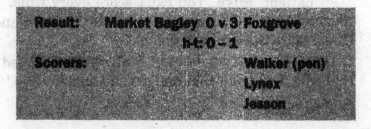

Result: Market Bagley 0 v 3 Foxgrove
                              h-t: 0 – 1
Scorers: Walker (pen)
                                  Lynex
                                  Jesson

GROUP TABLE

	P	W	D	L	Goals F	A	(GD)	Pts
Foxgrove	2	2	0	0	7	1	(+6)	6
Glendale	1	0	1	0	2	2	(0)	1
Mkt Bagley	2	0	1	1	2	5	(−3)	1
Teffield	1	0	0	1	1	4	(−3)	0

Note

Three points for a win, one point for a draw. If teams are level on points, their position is decided on goal difference (GD).

Analysis

The Foxes have plenty to celebrate, as you can see from the table above. They are five points clear at the top of the group already, but their place in the County Cup semi-finals is not yet assured. Glendale have a game in hand and the two teams have to play each other later in the term – at Glendale School. The Baggies are sadly out of contention now, although Teffield at the bottom can still catch the leaders up if they win both of their remaining matches.

... which team do you think are favourites to be Quarter Champions? ...

BOVVER BOY

... by the way, how's Carl settling in at Glendale, Mrs Burrows? ...

'This simply isn't good enough, Carl. I fear that if we have another incident of this kind, you may well find yourself suspended from school.'

Carl Simpson stared down at the yellow swirls of the headteacher's office carpet, not really listening to what Mrs Burrows was saying. The patterns reminded him of the pool of sick the dog had left overnight in the hall at home and he failed to suppress a giggle. His dad had stepped in it, barefoot.

'Are you finding this funny, young man?'

'No, Miss,' he replied automatically, struggling to keep a straight face.

'No, Mrs Burrows,' she corrected him. 'Then why are you sniggering?'

'I'm not, Miss . . . er . . . I mean, Mrs Burrows.'

The headteacher sighed heavily. Carl had arrived at Glendale with a very bad report from

46

his primary school and his continued antisocial behaviour was a cause of great concern to her staff.

'Your form tutor has done everything he can to try and help you, Carl,' Mrs Burrows continued, 'and now you reward him by swearing at him in front of the whole class. Such disgraceful language.'

Carl shuffled his feet through the imagined vomit.

'You ought to be ashamed of yourself, but I see quite clearly that you are not. Well, something has to be done to make you change your ways.'

Five minutes later, Carl slunk out of the office and down the corridor towards the playground. As he saw two of the footballers appear, he put on his usual defiant swagger.

'Have you been suspended?' Giant said, sounding hopeful.

'Nah, stupid old bat. Wish she had sent me home,' he said with a smirk. 'Would've been OK, that. Having a week or two in bed while you lot are still slaving away at school.'

'So what's happened?' asked Leggy.

'Just shown me the yellow card, that's all. One more and I'm off!'

'Nothing else?' said Giant, not masking his disappointment.

'Not much,' he said, scowling. 'Apart from being put in Fisher's form now. She seems to think that'll do me good for some reason.'

'I bet it's 'cos you're in his soccer squad,' said Leggy. 'Y'know, she probably hopes that Fisher can deal with you better.'

'Huh! Don't reckon he likes me much. Keeps making me sub.'

'Up to you to prove you're worth a place in the team, then,' said Giant. 'Show him that you're not just a clogger.'

'Are you calling me a clogger?'

'No,' he said quickly, having no wish to get into a brawl with Carl. 'I'm just saying that the more you kick the ball and not the man, the more he'll like it – and you.'

'Yeah, well, I'm not bothered, anyway. Who cares whether I'm picked or not? You guys don't.'

Despite his bravado, the rest of the squad saw how much Carl really did care about his football at their next practice session. When Mr Fisher caused a surprise by naming him in the starting line-up for the County Cup match at Teffield, Carl let out a delighted whoop and punched the air.

'Glad to see you're so pleased about playing,' the teacher said to him afterwards. 'If you can control that aggression of yours and channel it for the good of the team, you might be able to start earning youself a better reputation at the school. Think about it, eh?'

It was just as well for Carl that Mr Fisher didn't follow him into the changing room straight away. Alex Wainwright had been the unlucky one left out of the side and made some ill-timed, unflattering remark about his replacement as Carl walked through the door.

Before anyone could make a move to stop him, Carl dashed forward and punched Wainy hard in the stomach. 'That'll teach you, squirt, to call me a moron,' he fumed as his victim crumpled to the floor.

Paul dragged Carl away as others helped Wainy up onto the bench. 'You touch him again and I'll report it to Fisher. You hear me?'

Carl yanked himself free of the captain's grip and Paul thought for a moment that he was going to get thumped as well. Then he saw the fire die in the bully's eyes.

'Tell-tale, are you?' Carl sneered.

'No, just looking after my teammates.'

'Well I'm one of them too, remember.'

'Fisher's coming!' Crackers called out, keeping watch at the door.

When the teacher finally arrived on the scene, the tense atmosphere had eased and he had no idea what had happened.

'About time you people were making tracks home,' he said, before noticing the figure hunched over on the bench. 'Are you OK, Alex?'

The boy looked up, white-faced, and nodded. 'Just got a bit of gut-ache, that's all. Something's made me feel sick.'

TEFFIELD v GLENDALE

Saturday 8 November
k.o. 9.30 a.m.
Referee: Mr J. Pearson

*. . . Glendale are 3–1 up at half-time and look on
course for a comfortable victory – but then Carl
sees red . . .*

The start of the second half saw the best
and the worst of Carl Simpson.

He began it by increasing Glendale's lead
with a powerful drive that left the Teffield goalkeeper grovelling by the foot of the post, well
beaten.

After his boisterous celebrations were over,
Carl then went and spoilt all his previous good
work in the game. He did a crude two-footed
tackle on Andy Turner, showing his studs, just
as the attacker was poised to shoot.

The so-called Medd, Liam's father, was heard
again on the touchline. 'Off! Off! Off!' he
chanted, encouraging several young spectators
nearby to join in.

The home school referee, Mr Pearson, was not
responding to those biased appeals when he gave

Carl his marching orders a few moments later. It was a direct result of being subjected to a tirade of abuse from the boy after awarding Teffield a penalty for the foul. Carl's basic message that it was outside the box was lost among all the swearing.

It even seemed that Carl was going to refuse to leave the field until Paul steered him away towards Mr Fisher. 'Get off, Carl, before you make things even worse – for you and the rest of us,' he hissed. 'The ref might abandon the game and make his own team the winners.'

The referee went over to explain his actions to his fellow teacher. 'Sorry, Brian, I had to do it. The foul was bad enough, but I'm not going to have a boy swearing at me like he did. Got to set an example to the others.'

'Of course you have, I totally agree,' Mr Fisher said. 'Nobody should have to put up with that sort of thing. I'm sorry, we're having all sorts of problems with that lad at school. Leave him to me now.'

As the Teffield captain, Jack Whitehead, prepared to take the penalty kick, Mr Fisher wasn't even watching. He was giving Carl a lecture away from the pitch before sending him back to the cloakroom area.

'Go and get changed and wait for us in there,' he said bitterly, trying to control his own temper in public. 'I'll deal with you at school on Monday morning. You've gone and let everybody down, I hope you realize that, not just yourself. This was your last chance.'

Wainy, one of the substitutes, was listening gleefully to every word. 'Serves him right,' he chuckled. 'Reckon that moron will get a double suspension now – banned from football and from school!'

Carl stormed away and made a dent in the cloakroom door as he kicked it wide open. 'They're all against me,' he fumed, tears stinging his eyes. ' "Last chance," he says. Huh! Well, I'm not gonna miss this chance.'

He tore off his muddy boots and threw them against the wall. Then he started to go round all the coats, dipping his hands into the pockets to see what he could find.

. . . Carl's clearly bringing even more trouble upon himself, but are Glendale going to pay the penalty as well for his crimes? . . .

53

. . . let's hear striker Chris Kemp's account of what happened in the match . . .

One of the features of year group assemblies on Tuesdays at Glendale Community School was for a member of the football team to read out a report of a recent game. It was intended to be an honour, but the players saw it as something of an embarrassing ordeal.

Chris Kemp's reward for his hat-trick against Teffield was double-edged. There was the pleasure of being named *Man of the Match* by Mr Fisher, but also the dubious privilege of having to stand up in front of about two hundred people and give his account of their victory.

Chris had spent hours drafting and redrafting his effort until he was reasonably happy with it. Now, though, as he sat on the floor of the Year 7 assembly room, he broke out into a cold

54

sweat. Reading it through to himself in a desperate last-minute rehearsal, it sounded awful.

Then his name was announced and he glanced up at the P.E. teacher as if to plead for mercy. It was to no avail. Mr Fisher gave him the nod and Chris knew he was doomed.

'Good luck, Kempy,' whispered Paul, grinning. 'Make sure you tell everybody exactly what Carl said!'

Chris scrambled clumsily to his feet and picked his way towards the front of the room on what felt like borrowed legs. Head down, avoiding the sea of faces that were staring at him, he coughed and began to read nervously, aware of the paper shaking in his hands.

'This was Glendale's second game in the County Cup and . . .'

'Speak up, Chris, please,' Mr Fisher interrupted. 'Don't mumble.'

'Er . . . we needed to win to stand any chance of finishing top of our group, but Teffield gave us a shock right at the start when Crackers let a goal in through his legs . . .'

Crackers suddenly felt the sea washing in his direction and he turned a bright shade of crimson. 'Huh! Bet Kempy won't mention any

55

of the saves I made in the game,' he muttered to Dipesh Patel sitting next to him.

'He'd better give me a namecheck for my goal or there'll be trouble,' Dips whispered. Chris was gabbling on so quickly, Dips almost missed it.

'. . . After I equalized, Dips got his first of the season from long-range and then I put us 3–1 up at half-time,' Chris went on as modestly as he could. He didn't want to sound big-headed about his goals.

He risked a quick peek away from his script as he paused for breath. They were all watching him intently and he sensed their anticipation of how he was going to describe Carl's dismissal. Chris had two versions ready to use, depending upon whether or not Carl was in the audience.

Carl was absent. He hadn't even turned up at school yesterday and no decision had yet been taken about his likely suspension. Mrs Burrows wanted to speak to the boy's parents first.

'We played nearly the whole of the second half with only ten men,' Chris read out, feeling more confident. 'But it was a great team effort, battling to make sure we didn't throw away our deserved victory after Carl went berserk at the ref and stupidly got himself sent off . . .'

There were sniggers around the room at such

blatant criticism, knowing Carl would get to hear about it sooner or later. Chris realized that fact and wisely made a point of praising Carl's goal as well.

'. . . Anyway, Crackers saved the spot-kick but he was unlucky that their captain blasted home the rebound to make it 4–2. After that, we had a lot of defending to do, but Paul and Batty were on great form and the closest Teffield came to scoring was when they hit the post. We clinched things with our fifth goal near the end. Harry Taylor could have scored himself, but he passed it to me instead so I could complete my hat-trick. Thanks, Giant!'

Chris looked up and grinned as he finished on a high note. 'So that was it, and now only the Foxes can stop us becoming Quarter Champions. Come and cheer us on against them soon in the deciding game!'

He scurried back to his place to a loud round of applause. 'Phew! Glad that's over,' he said in relief to those around him. 'Don't reckon I want to be *Man of the Match* again this season!'

Result:	Teffield 2 v 5	Glendale
	h-t: 1 – 3	
Scorers:	Turner	Kemp (3)
	Whitehead	Patel
		Simpson

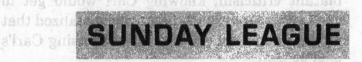

SUNDAY LEAGUE

. . . news travels fast – wonder how the Foxes are feeling now that Glendale have narrowed the gap at the top? . . .

When Mr Norton, Foxgrove's soccer coach, pinned up the latest group table on the Year 7 noticeboard, it soon became the centre of attention. The footballers gave it far more intensive study than any of their schoolwork.

GROUP TABLE

	P	W	D	L	F	A	(GD)	Pts
					Goals			
Foxgrove	2	2	0	0	7	1	(+6)	6
Glendale	2	1	1	0	7	4	(+3)	4
Mkt Bagley	2	0	1	1	2	5	(−3)	1
Teffield	2	0	0	2	3	9	(−6)	0

'Already knew Glendale had stuffed Teffield,' said Lynx. 'Liam told me before United's game last Sunday. 'Y'know, the Medd's kid – remember?'

'Who could forget the Medd?' Graeme smirked. 'Bet he made sure everybody knew what he thought about Teffield being knocked out the Cup.'

'It's just between us and Glendale now,' said Will Harrison, the left-winger. 'Guessed it'd work out like that. Some of them are teammates of mine on Sundays for Rangers. They won't half give me some stick if they beat us.'

'Well, they're not going to, are they?' replied the captain. 'We're the favourites. We only need a draw to be Quarter Champions.'

'Yeah, but they're at home,' Will pointed out pessimistically.

'So what? Doesn't make much difference at our age. They're not exactly going to have fifty thousand fans roaring them on, are they?'

Will shrugged. 'I'm just saying it's going to be tough, that's all. I mean, their guys are really up for it.'

'No more than us,' Graeme insisted. 'And you can tell your gang from Glendale on Sunday we didn't put out a full team when we thrashed them in that pre-season friendly. That should shut 'em up for a bit.'

The boys laughed. 'I'll make sure they get the message as well,' Lynx grinned. 'United meet Rangers this weekend and we've also got a Glendale player now. He joined us a couple of weeks ago.'

'Who's that?'

'Nick Green, their right-winger. He looks pretty useful.'

'Hmm,' murmured the captain thoughtfully. 'Could come in handy, this, with you two knowing so many of their players. You can point out some of their weaknesses and that. In fact, I might come along and spy on them myself this Sunday. My own team haven't got a game.'

'At least Glendale won't have their destroyer when we play them,' said Will.

'Destroyer?'

'Yeah, some thug called Carl. Even the Glendale lads can't stand him. He got sent off against Teffield and he's been banned from playing football till the end of term!'

When Graeme turned up at the recreation ground in the village of Dunthorpe, about halfway between Glendale and Foxgrove, he knew that it was the right place as soon as he climbed out of the car. The Medd's angry shouts were echoing off the walls of the changing cabin.

'United must be losing,' Graeme joked to his dad.

That wasn't the case in fact. They discovered that the visitors were already 2–0 up against Dunthorpe Rangers. The Medd just loved to moan. Graeme spotted a mate on the touchline and went over to him.

'What are you doing in your trackie, Zed? Thought you were a regular for United.'

'I am. I get more games for United than I do for school. Just got a kick on the knee and had to come off.'

'Who did that to you?'

Zahir Aziz pulled a face. 'That little kid over there in midfield,' he said, pointing. 'One of the Glendale lot, I think. Heard Will call him Wainy.'

'Obviously not the Destroyer, that size, is he?' Graeme chuckled. 'Are you gonna be OK for the big match, Zed?'

'Sure. Just a knock, that's all. I'll be fit again in time – if I'm needed.'

'Has Lynx scored?'

'No, but he made the first goal. Took it brilliantly, Nick did, hit it right in the bottom corner. That's Nick on the ball now, the number seven.'

Graeme watched the winger with interest. 'Hmm, not as fast as Clayton, but he'd still take some catching if he was allowed a run at goal.'

Nick managed to get another shot on target before half-time, but this one was held by the Rangers goalkeeper, another Glendale teammate. David Nash wasn't beaten again until deep into the second half when Lynx slipped the ball past him from close range to clinch United's victory.

'Bad luck, Will,' Graeme said as the teams trooped off the pitch.

'Huh! I had a real stinker today.'

'Well, not to worry, the Glendale people weren't up to much either as far as I could tell.'

'Reckon we all had a bit of an off day.'

'Got to be good news for us, though,' Graeme grinned. 'If they're off form for Rangers, let's hope it affects Glendale too. That'd sure make our job easier in a fortnight.'

. . . there's one other game still to be played in the group as well, remember, between Market Bagley and Teffield – compare what the local papers have to say about it afterwards . . .

READ ALL ABOUT IT...

The BAGLEY BUGLE

Monday 24 November

BAGGIES MAKE UNLUCKY CUP EXIT

It's the end of the County Cup campaign for the Year 7 soccer team of Market Bagley Community School. The boys drew their final group game 1–1 with Teffield Comprehensive on Saturday morning to finish in third place.

The Baggies had much the better of the hard-fought draw and deserved to win the match. After a goal-less first half, with defences on top, they peppered the Teffield keeper with shots and headers but could only find the net once.

The visitors had gone ahead with a goal against the run of play, but the Baggies' equalizer was well worth waiting for. It was a magnificent header from centre-back Oliver Kane, his very first goal of the season.

'The lads have been unlucky in the Cup this term,' said their P.E. teacher, Mr Roger Knight. 'They've worked hard, but have not been able to turn enough chances into goals. I'm sure they will put this right in their league matches after Christmas.'

™THE TEFFIELD WEEKLY

THURSDAY 27 NOVEMBER

TEFFIELD ROBBED OF FINAL CUP VICTORY

Market Bagley 1 – 1 Teffield

Teffield School's under-12 soccer team were so unlucky not to win their last group game in the County Cup.

The boys needed a victory to lift them off the bottom of the table. They looked to have achieved this result when a controversial late goal was given against them, one of a series of bizarre decisions by the home school's referee. The scorer had clearly fouled the Teffield defender, Liam Hunter, as they jumped for the ball together, causing tempers to flare among the parents on the touchline.

'It was a pity it had to end that way,' said the Teffield P.E. teacher, Mr Jeff Pearson. 'The lads were well on top right through the game and should have won by a wide margin.'

The goal Teffield scored was a stunning, acrobatic strike by leading marksman, Andy Turner, from a centre by captain Jack Whitehead. Many more goals might have followed, too, if the Baggies keeper, Deacon, had not been on such good form.

Better luck next season, lads!

CUP STATS

TEFFIELD

Latest match

Result: Market Bagley 1 v 1 Teffield
h-t: 0 – 0
Scorers: Kane   Turner

GROUP TABLE

	P	W	D	L	F	A	(GD)	Pts
					Goals			
Foxgrove	2	2	0	0	7	1	(+6)	6
Glendale	2	1	1	0	7	4	(+3)	4
Mkt Bagley	3	0	2	1	3	6	(–3)	2
Teffield	3	0	1	2	4	10	(–6)	1

Analysis
Both Foxgrove and Glendale still have every-thing to play for in their final match against one another. Foxgrove need at least a draw to finish top of the table, but a victory for Glendale would

see them leapfrog over the Foxes and claim the title of Quarter Champions. Only the group winners qualify for the semi-final stage of the County Cup.

Leading Cup scorers

3 – **Jesson** (Foxgrove); **Kemp** (Glendale); **Turner** (Teffield)

2 – **Wilde** (Market Bagley)

IN TRAINING

. . . take a peek inside Glendale's sports hall where the soccer squad are sharpening up their skills – but why are there so few players to be seen? . . .

'I'll be OK for Saturday, no bother,' Crackers insisted whenever anybody asked about his ankle. 'Just needs a bit of rest, that's all.'

Glendale's regular goalkeeper was not taking much of an active part in the training session. He had hurt his ankle playing football at lunchtime. The injury could hardly have come at a worse time with the vital Cup game so close and the first-team squad already depleted through illness. Both Robbie Jones and Hanif Khan were off school sick and unlikely to return.

Despite the boy's assurance, Mr Fisher was a worried man. He was running short of players to choose from. If Crackers wasn't fit, David Nash was the obvious replacement, but the teacher preferred to play Nashy in midfield to take advantage of his stamina and strong tackling.

While the remaining members of the squad

split into small groups to work on various ball skills, Mr Fisher paired the two goalkeepers together. Crackers began by throwing the ball towards his understudy at different heights and angles so that Nashy could practise his handling technique.

'Heard that Nick put one past you the other Sunday,' he teased.

'Yeah, but I bet he didn't tell you what he said to me,' Nashy retorted with a grunt as he dived to smother the ball.

'What was that?'

'Said you were nasally challenged,' Nashy giggled. ''Cos you wouldn't have smelt another shot of his I saved later.'

'Charming!' Crackers snorted and then grinned. 'I'll get Carl to *do* him for me. Did you know he's a fan of yours, by the way?'

'Who, Nick?'

'No, I'm talking about Carl. He reckons you should be in goal, not me.'

'Come off it. He's no mate of mine. He's no mate of anybody's.'

'Well, perhaps he just hates you less than he does me!'

The next ball skidded underneath Nashy's body and hit the wall, rebounding to clip him on the side of the head. He slumped down to take a breather. 'Pity Carl's not available, though,' he reflected. 'I think we might need him against the Foxes. Especially now.'

Crackers shook his head. 'Nah, we're better off without him. You never know what he's going to do next. We played better as a team with ten men after he got sent off that time.'

Half an hour later, the session ended with a lively six-a-side game, with Crackers sitting up on the wallbars, acting as scorekeeper. Mr Fisher watched thoughtfully from the side as well, musing over team selection until he glanced at his watch.

'Right, finish off, lads,' he announced. 'Time to go home.'

'Have you decided who's playing?' asked the captain.

'Just about, but I think I'll sleep on it first,' he replied. 'We may have to switch to 4–3–3 to reinforce the midfield area. I'll tell you all what the team is tomorrow morning. Meeting at break, don't forget, lads.'

As if they would. Nobody wanted to miss the chance of playing in the 'Big One'.

COUNTY COACH

GOALKEEPING

A team needs players who can score goals – but it also needs somebody who can stop them. A good goalkeeper is behind every successful side.

Want to improve your own goalkeeping skills? Take a few tips from me.

✓ Concentrate on the game, not on spectators behind you

✓ Keep your eyes on the ball – expect the unexpected

✓ Get your body behind the line of the ball as an extra barrier

✓ Get your hands right behind the ball, fingers spread out

✓ Catching the ball is safer than just blocking it – no rebounds

✓ After catching the ball, bring it in towards your chest for safety

✓ Be ready to come off your line quickly to narrow the shooting angle

✓ Distribution – an accurate throw is often better than a hopeful kick

✓ Shout – organize and encourage your defence

✓ Keep practising

GREAT SAVE!!

TEAM SHEETS

The two teams for the final match in the group to decide the North Quarter Champions line up like this:

GLENDALE

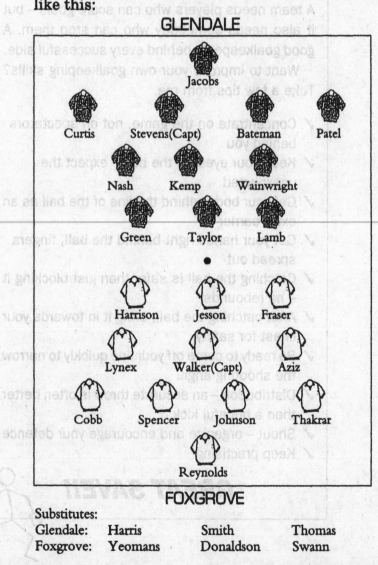

Jacobs

Curtis   Stevens(Capt)   Bateman   Patel

Nash   Kemp   Wainwright

Green   Taylor   Lamb

Harrison   Jesson   Fraser

Lynex   Walker(Capt)   Aziz

Cobb   Spencer   Johnson   Thakrar

Reynolds

FOXGROVE

Substitutes:
Glendale:	Harris	Smith	Thomas
Foxgrove:	Yeomans	Donaldson	Swann

GLENDALE v FOXGROVE

Saturday 29 November
k.o. 10 a.m.
Referee: Mr S. Murphy

. . . this is it – the 'Big One' – the most important match the boys have played in their lives is soon to kick off . . .

'**U**p the Foxes!'

'C'mon, lads, you can do it.'

The gold-shirted players received a great burst of cheers from their travelling supporters – parents, families and schoolmates – as they emerged from the changing room. Graeme Walker led the Foxes out, glad to feel the wind in his hair after the tense atmosphere inside. Even Sunday teammates had barely spoken a word to one another.

'Let's show everybody how we can really play,' he cried. 'Put on the style. We're the Champs!'

That wasn't strictly true – yet – but the school's name was the last one engraved on the large Quarter Shield that stood on a presentation table near the pitch. Foxgrove High had won the Year 7 Shield last season and Mr Norton was very keen to put it back in his car boot after the match and return it to fill the empty space in the school's trophy cabinet.

The goalkeeper's brother had been a member of that successful side, a fact that Matt was not allowed to forget. He took up his position in goal as a couple of players prepared to shoot in and give him a good feel of the ball.

'We've got to win today and retain the Shield, if only to shut my stupid brother up,' he called out. 'He'll make my life a misery otherwise.'

'We don't even have to beat them. A draw's enough,' Lynx reminded him. 'That's what makes us favourites.'

Mike Jesson was far more positive. 'We're not gonna mess about just playing for a draw. We're gonna thrash 'em!'

Mr Fisher kept the Glendale squad behind in the changing room for a few minutes before letting them loose. He made sure they all knew their positions in the changed line-up and what was expected of them. Crackers had declared himself fit to play, despite the teacher's misgivings.

'Just do your best,' he finished, 'and nobody can ask for anything more, whatever the final result, OK?'

There were nods all round. They knew the teacher wanted to win as much as they did. He was always in a bad mood at school after they lost.

'Who's the referee, Mr Fisher?' asked Crackers.

'Not me, I'm glad to say,' he replied. 'Can't afford to show any bias in a match like this. We've got a neutral referee, a Mr Murphy.'

'Saw him outside,' said Nick. 'Got all the proper gear on, he has. Looks dead official, y'know, not like . . .'

He stopped just in time.

'Not like me, you mean, in my scruffy old tracksuit,' Mr Fisher said with a grin. 'Right, Nicholas, I'll remember that in our next P.E. lesson. You can demonstrate to the rest of the class how to do twenty press-ups!'

The joke helped the boys to relax and sent them out in good spirits, eager for action. The home team enjoyed plenty of support themselves as they ran on to the pitch to warm up.

'Good luck, lads,' Paul's mother called out.

'I think they're going to need it,' murmured

Mr Stevens. 'Foxgrove are top of the northern schools' league as well!'

There was one person standing near the goal, however, whom the captain was not pleased to see – Carl Simpson. He'd been threatening all week to turn up and jeer.

'You ain't got a chance without me,' he taunted them. 'You're gonna get slaughtered!'

'Just shut it, Carl,' Paul retorted. 'Clear off back home if you've only come here to see us lose. You're supposed to be on our side.'

'The only side I'm on is mine, *captain*,' he sneered, before slouching away towards the corner flag as Mr Fisher approached.

Paul went up to shake hands with Graeme and the referee in the centre-circle. He won the toss and chose to shoot towards the school first, a popular decision among his teammates.

'We've got most of our goals at that end,' Giant pointed out.

'And it means we'll have the wind behind us second-half when we're getting tired,' added Batty, Paul's partner in central defence.

Straight from the kick-off, Graeme tested the wind's strength with a long-range punt at goal from only just inside the Glendale half. If he hoped to catch the goalkeeper by surprise, he was disappointed. His shot was powerful enough, but passed wide of the target.

His early effort, however, was not entirely wasted. As Crackers went to fetch the ball from the hedge behind the goal, Graeme noticed something.

'I think their keeper's limping,' he said to Mike. 'Did you see?'

Mike shook his head. 'No, but I'll soon find out. You watch.'

The Foxes' top scorer was as good as his word. He deliberately overhit a long pass too far in front of Clayton, but the winger's speed made Crackers move more quickly than he might have wished. He had to come out and gather up the loose ball on the edge of his area. His limp was obvious.

Crackers had his ankle tightly strapped for support, but it was still hurting more than he was prepared to admit. He rolled the ball out to Paul, not wanting to do any kicked clearances, and then called to his full-back. 'Don't give that guy a head start, Dips. He's like lightning.'

'Yeah, I've heard all about Clayton. I'll just have to make sure I get to the ball first.'

That was easier said than done. Trying to cut out a pass before it reached Clayton, Dips was beaten by the bounce of the ball and it left the winger clear down the touchline. There was no catching him now.

Clayton curled the ball into the goalmouth, but he had outpaced even his own teammates and nobody could reach it in time. The ball ran through to Will Harrison on the left side of the area. The number eleven controlled it quickly, took aim and fired. He was on the verge of screaming 'Goal!' when a green figure flashed across the goal-line and knocked the ball out for a corner.

'Fantastic save, Crackers!' cried Batty above the applause ringing around the pitch. 'How the hell did you get to that one?'

Crackers himself wasn't sure that he knew the answer. The save was based on pure instinct, but it was at a cost. As he stood up, the pain in his ankle was far worse than before.

Will stood shaking his head for a few moments, hands on hips, hardly able to believe that he hadn't scored. He left the job of taking the corner, as usual, to Lynx.

It began as a left-footed outswinger, but the wind caught hold of the ball in flight and swirled it back in towards goal. It defeated the lunges of several players in the crowded box and bobbled out of play past the far post. All it would have needed was a touch to send it into the net.

Glendale supporters and players breathed a collective sigh of relief at the escape. The pressure was off for the moment, but it was clear to everyone now that the goalkeeper was in some discomfort. Batty was taking the goal-kick for him.

There was no doubt either as to which team was on top for the first twenty minutes. The blustery wind made it difficult for Glendale at times to make much headway and Giant was often their only player left upfield. And even he came back into his own penalty area to use his height at corners.

Mr Fisher had never seen them defend in depth with so much determination to protect their goal – and their wounded goalie. The wide players, Nick and Leggy, tucked back into midfield and were sometimes found helping their own full-backs cope with the speed and skills of the opposing wingers.

So when the first goal of the match was finally scored, it came as a total shock. It went to Glendale.

Wainy won the ball deep inside his own half, dispossessing a tentative Zed who remembered his tackling from their Sunday encounter, and slipped it to Chris Kemp. Glendale's hat-trick hero from their previous Cup game had barely been over the halfway line yet and didn't make the journey now. But the ball did – very swiftly.

Chris swept it out to Leggy on the left, and the Foxes were caught on the break. As defenders hared after him in pursuit, Leggy switched play with a long cross over to the right where Nick was unmarked. Two touches later, the ball was nestling in the back of the Foxgrove net.

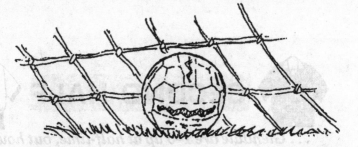

Matt was speechless at first, struck dumb by the outrage of the goal. But as Glendale celebrated, the keeper made up for his uncharacteristic silence and let rip at his shame-faced teammates.

'Where were you?' he screamed. 'I don't believe it. I was all on my own. You're useless.'

Matt was still fuming at half-time, but Mr Norton managed to calm him down and told his players not to panic.

'Let's see what you're made of now,' said the teacher. 'You don't deserve to be behind, but you are. So stop the bickering and get out there in the second half and put things right. It's up to you.'

'C'mon, we can still do it,' the captain urged. 'We only need a draw. Just one goal and that's it. Their luck can't hold out much longer, not with a crocked keeper . . .'

He was interrupted. 'Look over there,' said Will, pointing to the Glendale camp. 'That kid's coming off. Nashy's pulling his goalie top on!'

81

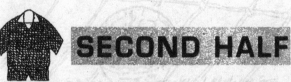

SECOND HALF

... Glendale are 1–0 up at half-time, but how are they going to cope with the loss of their goalkeeper? ...

Crackers had been the star of the first half, making a number of outstanding saves to frustrate Foxgrove, but he was in no real fit state to carry on.

A minute before the break, he had parried a close-range shot and then scrambled across his goal to try and block the rebound. He failed. His ankle gave way and he crumpled to the ground, helpless, as the ball was scooped over the crossbar by an attacker.

'The longer you try and play on, the more you risk making the damage worse,' Mr Fisher pointed out as Crackers protested about being substituted. 'You might even have to miss the rest of the season. How would you feel then?'

Put like that, Crackers could only shrug and accept the decision. He knew it was right. In a way, it was a relief to be able to go and sit down on the bank next to the pitch. His ankle felt as if a dog was gnawing at the bone.

David Nash had come prepared. The new keeper collected his own pair of goalie gloves from the sports bag he'd left with his dad on the touchline. They were still dirty from the last Rangers game.

'Big effort again,' the captain demanded, shaking his fists at his teammates as they prepared to restart the game. 'If we can hold on to this lead, we'll be Quarter Champions in half an hour.'

That sounded a very long time away. Even though the wind was now at their backs, the Glendale players were fully expecting the bombardment to continue – and they were right. The Foxes immediately poured on to the attack down both wings in search of the equalizer, forcing Nashy into action twice. He got his body in the way of a blaster from Mike Jesson and then dived bravely at Will's feet to rob the winger of the ball.

Will sportingly helped his Rangers teammate up and checked that he was all right.

'Thanks, I'm fine,' Nashy grinned. 'I can't let you score, of all people.'

'Plenty of time yet, Nashy. We've scored in every match this season. Nobody's kept a clean sheet against us.'

'There's always a first time.'

Glendale survived the storm and gradually began to put together some promising moves of their own. They enjoyed their best spell of the match during the next ten minutes, the wind helping them to keep the visitors' defence busy for a change. Matt was called upon to make saves from Chris and Leggy before Nick aimed another high cross towards Giant's head.

Matt reached it first, taking control of his own goal area and confident enough, as always, to  catch the ball rather than punch or tip it away. He seemed to have it in his grasp and then suddenly it was gone, spilled at the feet of the gangling striker.

Before either Matt or any defender could recover, Giant had poked the ball over the line from five metres out to put his side 2–0 ahead. The goalkeeper squatted on his haunches and closed his eyes in anguish, trying to avoid the accusing stares of his teammates – but he was only too aware of a familiar, sniggering voice behind him.

'Oh dear, that's gone and done it, little brother. Who you going to blame for letting that one in, eh?'

To their credit, his defenders resisted the temptation to exact their revenge and add to the goalkeeper's misery. It was Bread Roll who fished the ball out of the netting and hoofed it upfield for the restart.

'Forget it, Matt,' he said. 'Just one of them things. We all make mistakes, I guess.'

'I don't . . .' said Matt weakly, his face as white as a sick note.

'C'mon, team, don't give up,' urged the Foxes captain. 'It's not over yet. We've gotta fight our way back into this game.'

Graeme Walker took it upon himself to inspire a comeback. Playing a neat one-two with Clayton up the right, he beat Batty for pace and fired a shot at goal in his stride. Its power surprised Nashy, but he managed to get a glove on the ball and deflect it against the post.

The near-miss gave the Foxes fresh hope and

both Zed and Lynx went close, too, as the group leaders piled on the pressure. Deservedly, they gained their reward at last when Paul was too slow clearing the ball from a corner and had it whipped off his toes. It caused a panicky scramble in the goalmouth that saw the ball kicked off the line before Mike hooked it past Nashy into the top corner of the net.

The Foxes didn't even bother with their customary celebrations. Time was too precious to waste on the 'foxhunt'.

'How long to go, ref?' Graeme asked.

The official glanced at his watch. 'Oh – five minutes at least.'

'Five minutes!' the captain yelled so that everyone knew the situation. 'C'mon, they've cracked now. Another goal will do it.'

The supporters of both sides had rarely known a more nerve-racking five minutes. To Glendale, they seemed to last for ever. To Foxgrove, the hands on their watches were whizzing around the dials like speedskaters. The two teachers, standing just ten metres apart, caught each other's eye and grinned.

'Still up for grabs,' said Mr Fisher.

'Aye, it only takes one kick to score a goal, as they say,' replied Mr Norton. He decided to throw caution to the wind and waved his defence forward. It didn't really matter now whether they lost 2–1 or 6–1. It was the equalizer or nothing.

They almost paid the price for such a gamble. A huge clearance from Batty sent Leggy clear again, just like for the first goal. This time Leggy was on his own, racing towards Matt who was coming steadily out to meet him. The winger thought about trying to dribble round the keeper, thought about it again, and then lobbed the ball goalwards instead.

Everyone watched the ball's flight. It looped high and dipped suddenly, landing gently on the roof of the netting. A few centimetres lower and the contest would have been all over – but not now, not yet.

The referee kept checking his watch as Foxgrove forced two corners in the final minute. Lynx swung both across with deadly accuracy and even Matt came up for the second one, adding to the crush in the Glendale goalmouth. He and Mike jumped for the ball together against Giant, but the beanpole striker headed clear.

The ball fell to Graeme, lurking in a little space just outside the penalty area. He struck the ball on the volley as it dropped and hammered it through the forest of bodies.

Nashy never even saw it coming until the last split second . . .

The cheers erupted on the touchline and they were still echoing around the pitch when the referee blew his whistle, waving his arms in the air to signal the end of the match. The reactions and emotions of the players were in stark contrast. Spirits soared and dreams died in the very same instant.

'What a game!' one of them shrieked at the top of his voice in excitement. 'What a game!'

Nobody was going to argue with that – win, lose or draw.

Several minutes later, the victorious captain was handed the Quarter Shield and he held it proudly above his head to generous applause from the two sets of supporters. Both captains had been secretly rehearsing that traditional act at home the previous night – Paul with a large jug in his bedroom and Graeme with a teapot in the kitchen.

But only one of them now savoured the moment for real.

It felt magic!

. . . so who do you think has lifted the Shield? Did that last shot go in or not? Turn over the page – when you're ready – to see if you are right . . .

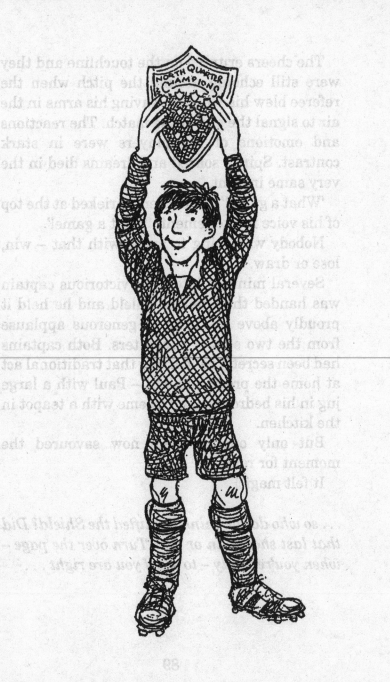

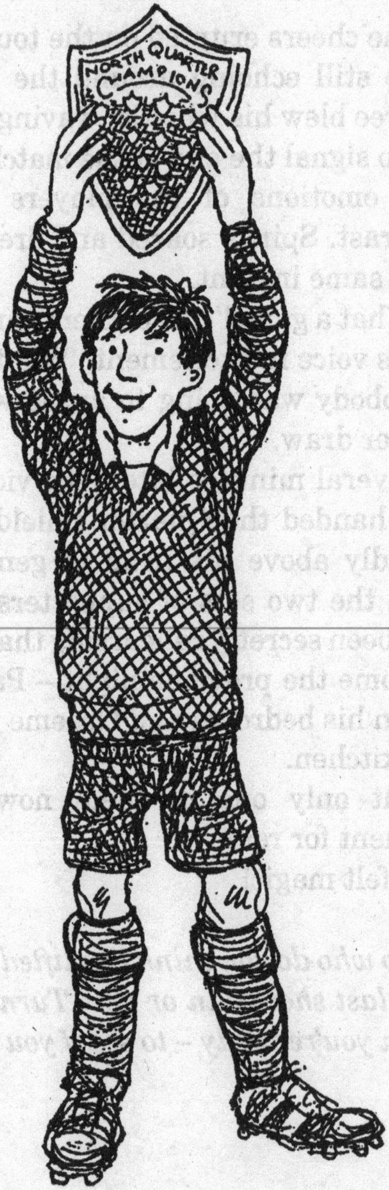
NORTH QUARTER
CHAMPIONS

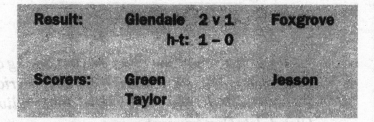

Result:	Glendale 2 v 1	Foxgrove
	h-t: 1 – 0	
Scorers:	Green	Jesson
	Taylor	

MATCH STATS

Nashy's dad kept a record during the game of all the relevant facts and figures. He liked doing that sort of thing when his son was playing. He gave the final statistics to Nashy to take into school and show everybody.

	GLENDALE	FOXGROVE
Goals	2	1
Shots	7	15
Headers	4	3
Saves – (Crackers)	6	5
– (David)	8	
Corners	4	9
Fouls	3	3
Offsides	1	4

POSTSCRIPT

. . . scene: it's breaktime on Monday morning and three footballers are in the school corridor, taking shelter from the rain and reliving Glendale's Cup triumph . . .

'What a save!' exclaimed Chris Kemp for about the millionth time since Saturday morning. 'A real blinder!'

'Won us the match, no doubt about it,' admitted Crackers. 'From where I was up on the bank, it looked a cert goal.'

Nashy grinned. 'The ball just hit me,' he said modestly. 'Didn't really know much about it – I was unsighted.'

'Told you it was a blinder!' Chris laughed. 'The ball took a deflection as well, I reckon, before you knocked it over the bar.'

'Well, anyway, don't forget all Crackers' saves in the first half. We might have lost the game by half-time if it wasn't for him.'

'That's why Fisher made both of you joint *Man of the Match*,' Chris said and then gave a smirk. 'Glad I can sit back and watch you two suffer in assembly tomorrow.'

'No chance. I bet Fisher will have all of us standing up at the front to show off the Shield.'

'Wonder who we'll draw in the semi-finals?' said Crackers.

Chris shrugged. 'Gonna be tough, whoever it is, East, West or South.'

'Oh, oh! Watch out!' Nashy hissed. 'Don't look round now, but here comes trouble from another direction.'

Carl sauntered up to join them. 'You lot were dead lucky on Saturday,' he sneered. 'Foxes should've scored about ten.'

'That's why a football team has a goalkeeper,' said Crackers. 'To keep all the shots out.'

'Oh yeah, very funny. Surprised Fisher didn't stick you both in goal at the same time.'

'Didn't need to,' said Chris. 'They're each good enough to do the job on their own.'

'Huh!' Carl snorted, fixing his glare on Crackers. 'How's the ankle, then, hero? Which one is it that's knackered?'

'The right. Still hurts a bit, but it's . . .'

'This one, you mean?' Carl cut in and gave it a fierce kick. 'Just there?'

Crackers collapsed to the floor, crying out in pain, but Carl's fists were already raised as the other two made a move towards him.

'Come on, then, have a go, I dare you,' he snarled as the boys checked their advance, wisely refusing the challenge.

'What did you do that for?' demanded Chris as Nashy bent over Crackers.

'He had it coming to him,' the bully sneered. 'Always trying to cheek me, he is. Well, he won't do it again in a hurry.'

Carl stalked off out into the rain, leaving them to support Crackers as he climbed unsteadily to his feet and limped over to a chair.

'We can't just keep letting him get away with things like that,' muttered Nashy.

'Who's going to stop him?' said Chris, shaking his head. 'Imagine having to put up with that maniac in the team again next term.'

Nashy groaned. 'Knowing him, he might even deliberately try and make us lose in the semi-finals, just to get his own back for everything.'

'Don't worry, I'll see that it won't come to that,' grunted Crackers, rubbing his throbbing ankle. 'Don't know how yet, but I will. I'm not gonna have Carl messing up our chances to win the County Cup.'

. . . wonder what will happen when Carl is allowed to start playing football again? How do you think the other players will react? Sounds like big trouble!

APPENDIX

RESULTS

Foxgrove	4 v 1	Teffield
Glendale	2 v 2	Mkt Bagley
Mkt Bagley	0 v 3	Foxgrove
Teffield	2 v 5	Glendale
Mkt Bagley	1 v 1	Teffield
Glendale	2 v 1	Foxgrove

FINAL GROUP TABLE

	P	W	D	L	Goals F	A	(GD)	Pts
Glendale	3	2	1	0	9	5	(+4)	7
Foxgrove	3	2	0	1	8	3	(+5)	6
Mkt Bagley	3	0	2	1	3	6	(−3)	2
Teffield	3	0	1	2	4	10	(−6)	1

Glendale Community School are the Champions of the North Quarter and qualify for the two-legged, semi-final stage of the County Cup.

GOALS

A total of 24 goals were scored in the six group games, averaging four per match. These were the goalscorers for each school:

GLENDALE

3 – Kemp
2 – Taylor
1 – Green, Khan, Patel, Simpson

FOXGROVE

4 – Jesson
1 – Harrison, Lynex, Walker
+ 1 own goal

MARKET BAGLEY

2 – Wilde
1 – Kane

TEFFIELD

3 – Turner
1 – Whitehead